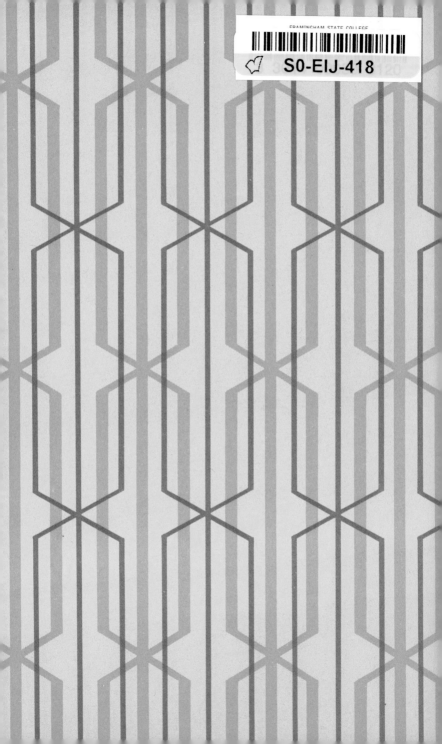

HYACINTH FROM LIMBO

HYACINTH FROM LIMBO

AND OTHER STORIES

by

Jean Rogers Smith

Short Story Index Reprint Series

BOOKS FOR LIBRARIES PRESS
FREEPORT, NEW YORK

For my brother Clinton

STANDARD BOOK NUMBER:
8369-3026-6

LIBRARY OF CONGRESS CATALOG CARD NUMBER:
76-81274

MANUFACTURED BY
HALLMARK LITHOGRAPHERS, INC.
IN THE U.S.A.

CONTENTS

HYACINTH FROM LIMBO

It was the day of the auction that I had at last found the chance to satisfy some part of an old curiosity. In the whimsical mood of the day, I concealed myself behind an ivory filigree screen on the plump pinkness of an ornately-carved bit of Victoriana, a love seat which Hyacinth had painted in punctilious naturalism—red, white, and pink roses with green leaves, nostalgic reminder of the romanticism of our girlhood. From this shelter in the great dark hallway, I could see the passionate yellow-greens burgeoning beyond the door and to the other side, the stairs. Those stairs! On them it had happened and those who would come today who had heard of it or remembered would be discreetly vigilant recalling their uncanny malevolence.

There had been many stories about Hyacinth, yet only one was irrefutable, and it was this one which had been most amusing to the naive and delicious to the vengeful while remaining the certain tragedy of her life. Raven, the eternal heretic, pronounced it a triumph, however, contending that she would play villainess upon a stage, or clown, rather than be ignored. Yet what did we know of her? what especially of these recent years since it happened and she had shut herself off from our little world? That she had enemies was apparent; you would expect it without the certainty that there would be friends.

Despite malice, there was also pride and affection, for we had re-conceived her; one, she had become many and each more real than life, a saga heroine, she had become scapegoat and wildest dream. Each saw his own desire beyond his changeling window-mirror.

On such a high spring hyacinthian day might that boy of eighteen perhaps who had never known her, intrigued by the rare whimsy of her pink and open door, hope to divine the substance of her life? Would not age itself be bewildered by such a place? And how many others had not come as he—ostensibly to buy such passionately feminine fantasies as few homes could stomach among their oak parlors and dingy vestibules?

Why, then, had they come? Was not her home fabulous and, to many, beautiful, or dare one suspect some appeal in the curious notoriety of her name? Surely, many a romantic had smiled hearing that old pied piper, the ancient music box, sing him a lorelei beneath the pudgy hand of a blond cherub, escaped from an antique-mad mama's eye or a gilded cupid frame, cranking obstinately away and perched on a stool. No, it was not all malice there!

One might easily wonder whether such extravagantly feminine decor had not beneath it some uneasiness of position, a rebuttal of a society which she might have imagined to have rejected her or the essence of her sex—her feminity itself. Certainly, there was something of the insult in these rooms? The pink vestibule, was it not a mockery of lasciviousness? a miniature Garden of Eden, the serpent concealed?

Madame arrived immediately after my taking sanctuary, and although I had not seen her since childhood, I recognized her at once by her massive entrance—chin pulled primly into triplicate, puffing under a towering plume, as she bristled into the room with that metronomic advance and stuffed-owl eye which, as children, we had imitated, turning our backs as she passed. I shuddered seeing her, sensing an indefinable omen in her arrival—a Virgilian harpy at the feast. Rigidly prompt, irritatingly methodical, she was nonetheless, a somewhat mythological character in that, although she referred to herself as Madame (for no accountable reason her name being Dutch), no one had ever seen her husband. Some said, not without facetious malice, that he had languished endless years in an institution (although of sound mind), to be rid of her. Who wished to be rid of whom was, of course, contested. Others claimed, as vehemently, that he was living across the hall with another woman —some said her mother. Another woman, who harbored an especial hatred, vowed that her husband ran a disorderly house of which she was headmistress. Of more reliable origin, perhaps, were the reports that she had the best funeral-attendance record in town, vying, no doubt with her mother who made ward history many years before while seated at a funeral, handkerchief at eye and bent in traditional grief, her stone-deafness defying the most frantic signals, as the chair beneath her played, "The Girl I Left Behind Me." Such were the milder rumors of her day.

An oyster behind the walrus, compact Mrs. Dunphy trod in upon Madame's wake, her rolling eye immediately transfixing the tortuous white hatrack and its cherry apples—faintly reminiscent of the forbidden fruit. Her dark face folded into contempt as she rounded the corner sniffing out the pantry, a treasure, and a scandal at one whiff.

Black Maria's great yellow eyes peering out from beneath his coat, the effete, and likewise modestly-whiskered Gerold slid into the hall. I might have missed his sinuous shadow had the exuberant Miss Schubert not wedged him back into the vestibule. Her ponderous presence, although of no romantic significance to him (indeed, had he ever eyed a woman with other than envy or disgust?), carried some artistic weight, for it was she who, for thirty years the idol of the music world, had sung of love and never known a moment of it, and he, the critic, had listened, and he must go on listening and she singing—offstage as well as on—nor ever might he mention should she wander from the pitch. They were squeezing the last drop of juice from the fruit, apparently, and as they passed en route for the living room, I thought I heard him sigh to himself, "L'Art pour l'Art" in the resigned tone of a drowning philosopher.

Evidently, the eyes of age and malice discerned properties alien to that young man who stood so thoughtfully before the tree of life, whose heart so visibly lifted at the sight, and may have been equally justified in judging its authoress to have been a joyous wit or a very sad woman attempting to be gay.

And then it was that I began to watch him, forgetting Hyacinth and the stairs and all that had come between in the many years since our friendship. There was an old sense of understanding, almost of temporary spiritual possession, a momentary reincarnation. I watched him as he moved from room to room, often disappearing behind the screen or beyond the outline of a doorway and drifting back again, stepping from rose to rose on the French carpet in abstraction like a child afraid to step on the lines of a sidewalk, staring into the watery darkness of a Venetian mirror, fingering its glass rosettes, and I knew, as suddenly as the ear knows the breaking of glass, that he was in love with her. How long could this bright dream last? Long enough, should he not probe reality. Immediately, I wanted it to last, to spare him disillusion. Better that she not come down those stairs again—incredible that it could happen all over again! Had he not heard them talking about her? Or did he not recognize of whom they spoke?

Madame and Mrs. Dunphy, turning from impatience to resignation, had set up a table and were playing cards as they talked, and when I turned my head over my shoulder, I could see through the doorway into the chandeliered and white living room where a maid was dipping scarlet punch from a crystal bowl. If they had begun in a whisper, one could not imagine it now. Surely he heard them, despite his turned back, as he traced the gilded grape and leaf of the delicate chair, as he stared at its white brocade!

"Vulgar taste. After IT happened, she let it run amuck—didn't care what they thought— appeared stark naked at the head of the stairs, her hair piled with crystal grapes when the new minister came to call, a charming bacchante, I'm sure!"

"And he?"

"Why, ran out, of course, and never bothered her for a penny after that."

"Hah! How naïve of you, Bertha!"

"Surely you don't believe Isobel, that Decline and Fall tale of hers?"

"Well, he wouldn't have been the first young minister to go astray in this town!"

"Oh, so you've heard that silly rumor of the young priest who ran off with the church money taking a juicy young nun with him!"

"I didn't have to hear *anything* to know more

about life and religion than you, Bertha! Dear, now you've made me forget what I was going to say. Oh, yes, Hyacinth; they say her mother was just as clever at getting rid of undesirables, dispensed with a tenacious old aunt who was coming for a winter's visit by whispering 'bedbugs' through the keyhole as she stood on the porch with ten suitcases. Speaking of the grapes, she had sort of an obsession with grapes, you know. Heard of the party she had where the centerpiece was ice and grapes? She had them passed at the end of the meal, let everyone make a fool of herself plucking some, then, rebuking them with a sly little smile, delicately wiped her fingers on the ice at the end—seems the grapes were just the decoration—a communal sort of finger bowl, you know."

"Why, no, Elsie. She hasn't left her room since IT happened. She couldn't bear the sight of those stairs again, never got over him, you know. After all, he *was* a terribly handsome man."

"We hear you sighing, Mabel. You were quite in love with Paul yourself, now, weren't you? Never mind protesting your age, and don't blush; your nose gets so red, and it just isn't becoming, and for God's sake, don't cry now! Sometimes I get sort of sick of that hypocritical charity of yours—just protesting to egg us on; don't think we haven't been on to that for years, my girl. Oh, I'm sorry, Mabel. I'm sorry! Anyway, as I said, you know perfectly well that Hyacinth *did* get over him; that girl from the gutter she deceived him into marrying pretending she was an old friend setting her up in style. . . . How she laughed in his face afterwards! Felicia! There was a plum, I tell you!"

Felicia had had the audacity to come and the misfortune to have heard. I could see her through the ivory lacework of the screen standing pink-faced beyond the staircase, a weasel-eyed blonde who, a moment before, had been bending over a Chinese bride's lantern. She had lit its candle, and the room was just dark enough for its light to cast butterflies of shadow through its filigree about the room. Her mouth had fallen open a bit, and her tongue licked back and forth across her upper lip in an old habit which I should never forget. And, then, I began remembering the past.

There had been a gala performance of the ballet at Swan's theater shortly after Felicia and Paul had been married, and I knew that he had already left her. Several of our group were talking in the hall during the promenade. Although it was rumored that he had been drinking heavily, he looked quite sober coming toward us that evening. Whether he ignored or simply didn't see us, I do not know, but suddenly, I heard him shout at someone behind us and as we turned, we saw that Felicia had been close behind us.

"Aha! Virgin Snyder! Loose again, I see." Felicia stood motionless as an animal playing dead, until the crowd moved on, her great colorless eyes filled with the pale yellow-green light of her satin gown while a voice whispered somewhere from the crowd, "Le diable, le diable."

While I had been remembering, Madame had evidently continued to pursue the theme, and her voice had risen a full octave. "Wouldn't live with her, you know. Always shouted 'virgin' at her when they met in public. Got so she was afraid to go out anymore. Suppose he made any more recluses out of feminine admirers beside Hyacinth and Felicia? I don't refer to plain old-fashioned broken hearts." She looked around meaningfully, secure in her seniority.

"Isobel will come, I expect. She always had the nerve! 'La Belle Dame Sans Merci.' In their laughter, was a bitterness beyond all humor.

What did I not recall? Who could forget the cruel and beautiful Isobel? Raven would twist

his satyr face and growl, "That female Iago!",
but rather than finding relief, as it usually delighted him to, in his fanciful comparisons of
literature to life, the mention of her seemed to
turn the screw deeper. Yet there had been a
time—soon after he had first come to live on
our street, moving into an apartment at Mrs.
Dunphy's—that she had had him in quite another
mood. It was Isobel's way to stalk her prey, yet
in so light-hearted and ingenuous a fashion as to
give the impression of a sweet innocence which
was invariably fatal to the equilibrium of the
masculine heart. To Mrs. Dunphy's vast annoy-
ance, Isobel would lean from her window and
call next door, "Come out of your ivory tower,
Raven. I'm in the most dire distress."

"Look at that pose, will you!" Mrs. Dunphy
would sneer. She fixed Isobel's scarlet-ribboned
black hair with a malignant eye, and when
Raven's grinning, quizzical face appeared at the
open window, she never failed to comment on
his unfortunate lack of intelligence. "There's experience in that face, I tell you. She's not the
first to make a fool of him! 'Isabella', he calls
her! The faithful Isabella who put her dead
lover's head in the Basil-pot, I suppose! If he
thinks she will be watering it with her tears and

dying for love of him, ah but he'll find out, poor boy. Pot him she will, though." And with this dire prophecy, she would go next door to complain to Isobel's mother that, although Isobel might look like the hanging gardens to her, this sort of ornamentation was most unwelcome. "I am not running a boarding house," she would offer, and then, pretending to change the subject, she would reminisce with relish a trip of her youth wherein "low" women leaned from their windows leering at men in the "colorful" sections of Algiers or stood outside their open doorways in chemises money being counted into their palms. Although you might think this would have been a great satisfaction to her, she was well aware that it was but "wind over the moon" (to use one of her favorite expressions). Isobel's mother, as Madame had so often reported, was "completely occupied making certain that nothing in her house had failed to have been painted lavender and that no letter had escaped with its invariable lavender stamp regardless of postage." And so, she stood, mild-eyed and preoccupied in the doorway, thinking, perhaps, how well her lavender dress looked with her prematurely white hair while Madame ranted at the moon.

This had been the happiest of all times for

each of us; Isobel had not yet turned our faces to the wall. But there were things to remember from the earlier years as well.

This house, whose early gloom I so well remembered, had been transposed to another key by Hyacinth's passion for color. It was one of an endless row spewed out by a lone architect in a lucrative hour—the only external sign of disorder, the jumbled numbering of the houses, caused by Hyacinth's mother who, upon her arrival, picked a number from her fancy, had it set in concrete, and imbedded in the house forever. So small an act did not make for an auspicious arrival; she was distinctly anachronistic to Primrose Street.

We lived in one of those "solid oak" interiors gilded by the fading light of the Victorian Age, and so like were they all, that we could find our way about conveniently in each other's homes. When we ate in our dining room, our neighbors could see our jaundiced faces, as we saw theirs, under the same ghastly green and yellow glass dome, hung from a great black chain. We climbed into each other's old ice boxes from identical green staircases or squeezed through the milk box when left keyless and forgotten by absent parents. And within, there were the same oak pillars and sliding doors that would not slide, the same hideous green tile-and-oak fireplaces, and often even the same white stuffed owl molting and dusty on the mantel.

A languid southern flower and self-styled belle, Hyacinth's mother was "a cochineal-haired, yellow-eyed vixen" in the estimation of such worthies as Madame. Her inevitable decay was prophesied somewhat prematurely by Mrs. Dunphy who ascribed it to moral turpitude and by my more tolerant mother as the natural consequence of the transplantation of a spirit accustomed to the warmth and sunlight of gallantry, now shut in by the dark, dank walls of respectability and the watchful eye of a suspicious husband.

It was Hallowe'en and my tenth birthday, when I first met Hyacinth. She came in white organdy festooned with lace, her carnelian hair in long curls. She was silent the whole evening, did not touch her cake nor bob for apples. Her great brown eyes looked out at us with that habitual terror and bewilderment which we, at first, mistook for pride. Isobel hated her immediately.

I did not see her again till spring when we all gathered on Isobel's porch to plan a play that we should put on, and when I was picked to direct it, she ran off and hid under the forsythia, cried and would not come out despite my pleading. "You may do it yourself," I begged, longing to lose a guilt unasked for which she refused to free me of and, ever since, when recalling it, have wondered which of us was wounded the longer.

Had it not been for a unique possession, none of us might have gone near her again. It was a large play house of gray stone surrounded by a high fence and secured by a padlock to which Hyacinth alone held the key, a miniature replica of any house on the street complete with kitchen and fireplace, a "last gasp Victorian or perhaps Presidential," as my mother used to say in alternate heat and unconcern. We played with her dolls but somehow not with her. In constant battle, most of them represented members of her family, but one (a boy doll with brilliant blue eyes and ruddy hair imported from Holland), must always play the fiend, and she subjected it to such constant tortures and humiliations, that it was soon an eyeless rag. It was a long time before I guessed who it was, and then one afternoon as I stared out the window and saw the Viking who came so often to see her mother, I knew. Perhaps had I not been so anxious to hide my own foolish rapture at sight of him in godlike progress towards us, I should have read her feelings earlier.

And so, in the sudden discovery of each other, we became friends. Reticence gave way to confession. She told me of her music teacher. "How she slaps my hands!" she cried. She often spoke, too, of her parents. "Mother never wanted me, you know. I heard Aunt Selda tell Daddy that she screamed and rolled on the floor to be rid of me, didn't want to spoil her figure," and she smiled with a trace of triumph. I tried to imagine Hyacinth's mother on the floor, but it was too incongruous. I did remember her not permitting her husband to shake salt on his food, "too provincial," and his laborious maneuvering of the tiny salt spoon and her distress when he leaned back in his chair as she smiled sarcastically, remarking, "I see you are making yourself very comfortable." But for me, she was eternally in the garden where I had seen her early one summer evening, a tiny, exquisite, and fastidious creature, a Boucher but for the color of her hair, nasturtium against a pink lace dress. She had murmured to Philip to wind the bird in that soft purr more willful than it sounded, and I recall his impassive expression as he did his wife's bidding as her lover, the momentarily handicapped Achilles, examined a leaf more closely than it deserved. The bird had been brought from France by Phillip, and it sang in remarkable imitation of the nightingale, turning its head as it sang in its brass cage. This "mechanism-upon-the-bough," as Raven leeringly called it in years to come, was ever a thing of fascination, and I had long dreamed that I might one day have it. After the others had gone indoors, I begged Hyacinth to let me play it again.

And so it sang over and over to my delight, now and then silent as a bird is silent, listening and waiting for the dark. Nor did I guess a reason for Hyacinth's unhappy look of patience until long after. Among the tokens of romanticism and sentiment with which Hyacinth's mother had surrounded herself, I especially recall the garden seat on which they had been sitting that evening. It was inscribed with a motto in Old French entwined with stone hearts and flowers: "One forgives all when one loves."

It was not long after that Hyacinth's mother ran away with her lover. The house was closed, and it was then that the stories began to come back which had so multiplied with the years:

that Hyacinth and her father had gone to live in Paris, that she had been terribly ill. Some said it was a mental illness, that she was in and out of institutions for years, had forgotten periods of her life, and, at times, even imagined herself to be someone else. I recalled how little she had liked herself and her life.

"I wish I were you," she had said, and I had laughed, "Surely, not so ordinary!" "I would like to be ordinary," she had sighed.

Some said that her father died of sorrow; others, of a dissolute life. And, of her mother, it was said that her lover had left her after a few years and run off with a French dancer and, later, that she had died grown hideously fat, leaving in her closets dozens of organdy petticoats with tiny waists. But Isobel, who had been in Geneva, claimed her to be still alive, that she had seen her on the street, had even recognized an old hat—hinting, in her sharp way, of a decay that evidenced no lady.

After her father died, Hyacinth and her Aunt returned, re-opening the old house. I did not see her at once being hopefully at work with my music and going daily to the Conservatory, but Isobel, always confident and sociable, pursued even those for whom she bore no affection and was soon dropping in to tell me of Hyacinth. It seemed, she was in love.

"Still having those secret passions," Isobel laughed, and her sharp little face lit up with glee, reminding me of a time when Hyacinth, at eleven, had conceived what Madame liked to refer to with relish as the "belle passion" for a young man who strode down the street from the direction of the Sen-Sen factory every weekday afternoon, his coat flying behind him and hatless in the fiercest weather, leaving in his wake a marvellously sweet smell. As we turned our noses to the wind in rapturous unison, Isobel whispered, "Get him, Hyacinth, and I'll take him away from you." Fate felt otherwise; the dream was pierced one Sunday afternoon when he chanced that way—followed by a plump wife and several plump children— quite innocent of the meaning of our stares and unmindful of Hyacinth's woeful face.

"How could I have guessed," she sobbed. "He didn't look like a married man. It's so unfair!" And she was unconsolable for several weeks.

Again I was back in the old house with Isobel as she talked about Hyacinth's new love. I could not see her face now, yet I knew it was no longer all delight; the delight was but prospect tarnished with misgiving. Her voice rose in my ear: "He

calls her 'Jacinthe' (French, he says, for Hyacinth), babbles about her 'jacinthian hair' (seems
it's a yellow-red stone); sounds horrid! Says she
should wear 'heavenly blue,' the color of the gem
'among the ancients.' And the posing! the affec-
tations! Can't go by now without hearing him
mournfully intoning Sappho from her garden.
Pan and his pipes! Someday I expect to find him
perched on a rock in a goatskin. Ugh! That ugly
face of his! Beauty and the beast; she thinks him
a foil to set her off, that voluptuous little serpent!"

"Some find Raven charming," I could not resist
replying. Isobel must have been looking down at
her fur scarf brushing off an imaginary fleck as
she so often did when silent and stalling for time.
"Animal magnetism, perhaps," she sneered at last.
I heard the chair crack softly; she was growing restless and began speaking half to herself
in that breathy way she had when excited, so
rapidly that I could barely understand her, ". . .
tell her legend Hyacinthus killed, struck by the
discuss, beautiful head bleeding, Spartan Hya-
cinthia festival of mourning, winter in the un-
derworld. Hyacinth flowers from blood in the
spring, 'alas!' on every petal . . . Blood, indeed!
And 'sweet' Hyacinth, alas!" Her mocking laugh
sped away. Gone in a mad triumph of plans,

she had not needed to tell me his name. Who but our beloved Raven?

I thought of Peredur in the Mabinogion as he stood in the snow looking at the dead fowl after the hawk who had killed it was frightened away and the raven stood over it, and of how he compared the red blood on the snow and the blackness of the bird to his love . . . But it was a matter of "Fox and Grapes" to Madame. As I passed her door, she eased her electric to the curb and, staggering out beneath a burden of bundles, accosted me, "She's playing her old games again!"

"Who?"

"Isobel, naturally. Passing around that Hyacinth has 'tainted' blood. Even got her to sing when Raven was there, frightful caterwauling, you know. Tone deaf." She hurried into the house in search of other ears.

The idyll was over. Through the long summer afternoons, Hyacinth sat in the garden, a book in her hand, and I could imagine, as I passed, the plaintive sound of the flute accompanying some ancient elegiac pentameters.

Daily, I promised myself that I would go to see her and, daily, delayed until one afternoon as I passed, she looked up and knew me. At sight of the childlike joy in her face I realized with shame

how lonely she had been. Going up the walk, I remembered her mother sitting on the landing window seat reading Lamartine and the bluish green halo about her flaming hair cast by the sunlight through the stained glass waves of the shipwreck scene that dappled the page and could imagine Hyacinth now drooping like the proverbial flower over Boethius' *Consolation of Philosophy* or *Le Roman de la Rose*. But she was gay and assured as I had never known her, with that hint of foreign accent which a traveller with a sensitive ear may acquire and lose in a few hours, which she had brought from we knew not where out of those eight years of absence. There was the same intensity about her that in childhood had so alienated the others, but her face, once a cameo of purity, had burgeoned in renascence as though at last reflecting the soul beneath, the rising bridge of her nose so reassembling the relationship of her features that at times I even imagined there to be something evil in the curious fixity of her eyes, somehow frustratingly elusive in the memory, as though she were a reincarnation of something disturbing—Coptic perhaps, a Christian martyr or a Savonarola, part of some memory of violence, perhaps. Yet as she spoke of the past and inquired about the present, it was with such innocent candor that I felt, with shame, that the "beam" had been in my own eye.

She told me of Paul and laughed, "He kept following us about, met him at the Prater in one of those little glass rooms on the ferris wheel, got stuck at the top for an hour with nothing to do but talk and stare down at the lights of Vienna; I thought I should be ill. And then one day on the Chiemsee in mad Ludwig's palace . . . At first, I imagined it to be a coincidence, as one travelling may meet a tourist in Pompeii and again in Florence and perhaps in a little boat on the Zuyder Zee and begin to feel a warm sympathy of shared centuries—even a possessiveness—only for him to disappear forever as one begins to expect him at the next town." And then she bubbled on about Paul a wine merchant, who drove a Mercedes-Benz and never smiled. I pictured immediately a demon lover, arrogant and the despair of all womanhood, smiling a "prosit" over a glass of wine and a candle in some ancient black-walled rathskeller.

"I have seen your 'rara avis,'" she sighed. Forgive the cliché; I have been so proselytized. Raven even claimed to know what my mother was reading before I was born! Sappho, of course! her 'purple hyacinth' trodden into the ground beneath

the shepherd's heel. He dwelt upon the insignifi-
cance of the ancient blossom, pitiful bluebell
size, unfortunate odor, but promised to plant a
little garden for me of scilla and other poor rela-
tions!" She rolled her eyes but looked as though
she might cry. As she fell silent, I knew she must
be recalling the white hyacinth for which her
mother had had so great a passion, whose fra-
grance had so filled the house in springtime. I
had often fancied that she had been blown away
on its high lyrical note, the "lark ascending" in
anguished ecstasy. Before leaving, I glanced at
the book under Hyacinth's arm; it was one of
those paper-covered French novels that one is
forbidden to bring into the country.

Yet of all the memories of my youth, I recall
most often the night of Hyacinth's engagement
party. It was spring. The windows were open and
the dark house was filled with candlelight. She
had asked me to come early and was waiting in
the hall. Her white gown cast up a lovely light
upon her face, yet I sensed that her flush of joy
was part fear. Standing behind her as she stared
at herself in the cupid mirror and adjusted a wisp
of hair, I wondered why so beautiful a girl should
be afraid of anyone, even Isobel. "Is she coming?"
I asked.

"Who would dare not invite the wicked fairy?" she cried. "You know, sometimes I lie awake at night imagining that she is one of the Medici reincarnated and will poison me with a ring, that she is passing me a cup of tea and I must drink it whether I like it or not, that she is saying incantations in a dark and smoky room while she sticks pins into my wax image, that I am helpless against her, growing ever weaker and soon must die. And then I dream that I am coming down the stairs against my will into the dark and cannot turn back and that someone is sitting down there in a chair facing me, and I dare not look at him for fear that I shall die from fear at sight of his loathsome grinning face nor dare go by without looking for fear he might spring up and kill me, and all the time I cannot tell whether he is dead or alive or which I'd rather have. Oh, why did there have to be a party? If only we had run away as Paul wanted to!"

"You could still go. How can I help you?" I was delighted at the thought of taking part in so romantic an event.

"Oh, Marie, it's too late! If you like, you might tell Isobel that Raven is about to inherit from his dear Aunt Agatha in Charleston."

"Or that Paul has some horrid ancestral disease, is dreadfully bourgeois anyway, eats with his fingers, smacks etc?"

"Better still, tell Mrs. Dunphy and tell her not to repeat it," she laughed wearily. But she seemed to be thinking of something else and during her disjointed talk seemed to have changed her mind —perhaps about confiding something to me. Yet when Paul came, I thought I knew, for he was one of those men who are at once heartbreakingly handsome and apparently unaware that it is so; she would always live in the fear of losing him, that someone cleverer or, someday, younger would entice him away, remembering too well, perhaps, her parents.

I recall watching them over Raven's shoulder as we danced. Too happy, I thought. Isobel was oddly silent. When the music stopped, someone suggested that we go out into the garden. It was a cool night and Hyacinth had gone up for a wrap. As we stood at the foot of the stairs waiting for her to come down, the Japanese lanterns were lit beyond the windows and the bird, which had been carried outdoors, began to sing. She appeared suddenly at the head of the stairs in a wide hat, smiling with delight, and as she drew nearer we could see that it was a fantasia of pink-feathered birds and feathery flowers startling against her red hair. What prompted this whim I shall never know, but in later years, Mrs. Dunphy still held out for "sadistic vanity," while Madame maintained it to have been "a preview of the honeymoon which she subconsciously knew could never be" and Raven, "a desire for self-destruction." Yet I do remember that Paul and Hyacinth looked only at each other in the ancient tradition of lovers. And what happened next so shocked us all that we never knew whether Isobel was surprised or not.

"Take it off Hyacinth," she whispered. "Don't make such a fool of yourself." She snatched the hat and the luxurious hair, which we had so long admired, came with it. Hyacinth stood motionless, as a figure at Madame Tussaud's, staring into the terrible present nor saw at all, I think, the shorn head in the cupid mirror readied for the guillotine. Someone began to laugh and was abruptly still. Her eyes dilated and she shivered. One moment it seemed she would come down upon us and the next that she would turn and run, but she stood paralyzed as by a terrible dream and it was we who, waking first, turned away to hear at last her slow feet upon the stairs moving as against the weight of a sea and from its depths, her waking cry.

This was the IT of which they spoke today, adopting a coquettish euphemism not extended to other of Hyacinth's adventures. One might almost hear the fluttering of fans veiling discreet smiles, a modern "Court of Love" in which, especially in masculine company, Madame, in referring to the location of her injury, would prudently spell "toe" rather than risk offending and, a moment later, refer to Felicia as a prostitute by a name less pretty.

The crowd had dwindled; outraged antiquers, having discovered that Hyacinth held no regard for so simple and straightforward a style as Early American, staggered dazed from the impact of so much raucous femininity.

"Insincere, insincere," a nettled feminine voice kept repeating as it faded into the distance. One bony woman in a smelly tweed departed twitching her nose and remarking, "There is no auction and she never intended having one. Just why did she bring us to this stinking mausoleum, this Malmaison?" I could see her starting down the street, her head eternally ahead of her body, raccoon eyes burning out beneath grey, matted hair, in search of the bluebird.

The singer and the critic passed the window

from the garden, and she seemed to be concealing something beneath the monstrous hulk
of her coat. It would be my beloved bird of
course. Stragglers who had been admiring the
garden came in, bringing their talk with them,
"Too sweet for my taste. . . ." Some, weary of
waiting, had gathered at a table and were gambling. Mrs. Dunphy and Madame, replete with
punch, were doing some gambling of another sort:
"She'll fling that crystal dressing table of hers
down the stairs or something with a Bacchic
touch perhaps." Madame closed one eye.

Raven, at last having found an innocent victim
for his endless discourses on genealogy, backed
the helpless young man into a corner and, punc-
tuating his remarks with a well-directed fore-
finger to the chest, reminisced upon the more
personal aspects of the family history.

"She was engaged to be married, you know. It
happened on the stairs. Everything in her family
happens on the stairs. Her Uncle was in a fire in
Kansas City, a hotel fire—thirty years ago, salesman, very thorough type, conscientious went back
to get his papers, last seen coming down the stairs
briefcase in hand. Disappeared in a cloud of
flame. Never seen again alive. Same with her
grandmother. Came from the old country, hus-

band a German immigrant went back to get her, wanted a wife from over there, 'one to work proper,' he said. Picture of them first married, frail little thing next to him. Up scrubbing before dawn though, scrubbed the outside of the house too, 'dawn to dusker.' he used to boast. He worked her hard. Sat around himself, had her cutting lawns, taking in washing, too. An executive type, he fancied himself. She got so strong that, hulk that he was, she threw him downstairs. Or perhaps he fell; no one ever knew as he was quite dead when they found him, a sort of male Amy Robsart case you might say." Raven smiled with a closed mouth in intellectual satisfaction. "And her cousin Eva, there's another. Stairs again. Spinster. Had some huge stairs she cranked up after her at night. Wealthy woman. Left all her money to her dog. And after all those years we played chess together!" He stopped, looking aggrieved.

Suddenly there was a shuffling sound above the stairs. One would have thought it too faint to arrest the talk of a roomful of people, yet so sensitive were the antennae of the watchful and curious. The young man paled and leaned against the wall. Raven stood at the foot of the stairs looking up, and it seemed for a moment that he stood out beyond the scene like a figure over an old-fashioned valentine, an auburn-mustached suitor in a lilac coat holding a bouquet, but immediately the chairs were crowding in around me, silently bidding for space. Madame, always first at the kill, was in front, knees spread apart, hunched forward, and peering upwards at the open space at the head of the stairs below the great orange-and-white silk Japanese lantern. What did each expect to see? There was that tense air of the séance, as though, like Dante's Bertran de Born, she might come through the Inferno carrying her own head before her as a lantern. What guilt had come in search of catharsis? of unconscious absolution? What of the large woman in the orthopedic shoes, mannish suit, and necktie whose bulging calf flattened as she crossed her knees, fingers fanning stiffly as she smoked, one of the Inner Sanctum perhaps? What of this sea of women in pink and lavender prints, so middle-aged, so firmly corseted, or the lady of thirty perhaps with the pink parasol and French gown of red silk, white and crystal beads against a brooding face reminiscent of a Renaissance painting—Isobel of course. But when had she come and how gotten in without my seeing her?

I stared at her glad of the shelter, not wishing her to see me, perhaps because I had not fared as well as she, perhaps afraid as one is forever afraid of a childhood enemy even when there is no longer reason. As I watched her, the gossip about Hyacinth began again; she too was, once more, "La Belle Dame Sans Merci." Quiet laughter as they eyed Felicia who sat clutching the bride's lantern—unwitting agent of Hyacinth's revenge?

"My corsetiere told me a friend knows her doctor, says the upstairs is filled with wild birds that fly about uncaged."

"Must have seen old Polly loose and multiplied her by a hundred. Hits the bottle a lot, you know. That upstairs! I'd like to get my hands on some of it, I tell you! She's kept the best up there, the sly little serpent—that sensuous thing by Courbet, woman on a couch with a parrot." . . . "In a museum you say? Well, the Boucher and Renoir I'm sure of—some of her euphemism, counterpoint on two floors. The upstairs is the same style—"

"Style? This hodge-podge style?"

"Well, you know what I mean, romantic. Venetian chandeliers with pink crystal roses and turquoise-blue flowers, pale pink carpets, French-white chairs. She wears ruby-red peignoirs. Odd with her red hair, don't you think? And she *has* gone out. My Myrtle has seen her walking the streets at night, wild-eyed with a white, haunted face. She's a frightened creature, a recluse, I tell you."

"Oh, Claire! What romantic nonsense! How can you believe all that?"

"Perhaps I don't; just making it up if you like," and she made a moue. "Going into a nunnery, then? What do you suggest?"

"Nunnery indeed! It's not so poetic, I tell you. Demi-monde is a pretty name for her. Elsa's heard from her friend at the telephone office that men call her late at night asking for a massage."

"Really, you're both outrageous. The rooms are quite bare, nothing in them but a row of wigs on faceless forms. Most of these people are bill collectors, back to get the goods if necessary. We'll be seeing her wigs about town on other heads, just watch. Why did you think she was having the auction anyway?"

"Well, who said she is? It was only a rumor."

"She may never come down, then."

Somehow, I think I had known it all the time. She would never come down.

The cupid was child, after all, and had fallen asleep over the music box, his feet on the scarlet seat of a French chair. What if he were mine? I could be blind and know him better, love him better than the others, for they would know him only by the warm yielding of his cheek, the eternal child-shape, the enchanting child-colors, but I should have nursed him at my breast and early learned his cries, his own fruity, sweet, animal and earthy scent that marked him as my own. And I should hold him as he slept and kiss him endlessly . . . Perhaps, when they had all gone, he would stay with me . . . But, in the end, it was Isobel who came to carry him away; she stood in the hall. The critic and the singer were there —not gone as I had thought. The bird began to sing a bit beneath her coat.

"Heu cuculus," Raven sighed, and Isobel stared at him with an angry smile to mock him.

"Quoth the Raven," she said.

"How is Paul, dear Isobel?" he asked.

She did not answer but, taking the child by the hand, started out, his sleepy head bobbing forward, his feet stumbling behind her. That Paul was dead, we all believed. Had Isobel herself not told us that he had broken his neck diving from a balcony into a fountain behind a hotel in Venice? "Quite drunk," she had said, implying that she had heard it all from a friend, but Raven had asked her sly questions, a disarming attorney for the prosecution, trapping and revealing her so publicly that she dared not mention him again.

"Wanton creature. Followed him over there as soon as he got rid of Felicia. His child; no doubt of it," proclaimed Madame looking up prudently beneath her great black eyebrows at Isobel's receding back.

They were all leaving now, and each seemed to feel he was quitting a stage and would turn to say a line as though he had rehearsed it for the occasion. The critic bowed to himself in the hatrack mirror, repeating himself with satisfaction: "L'Art pour l'Art." The young man had gone; when, I didn't know. How had it been for him? Unbelievable? Wildly beautiful at first? Incredible thought! Young man in love with old Hyacinth? No, not youth in love with age but with timelessness, like beings asleep in a land beyond pain or age or sorrow, as those in the Ancient Irish Tales who heard the music of Cormac's branch of silver with its golden apples or the women from Oxford who saw Marie Antoinette sitting in the garden of Versailles and heard her playing her harp centuries after she had died. So Hyacinth. Had she been old and ugly—even diseased—no barrier. And had he not run sickened yet joyful from the house? eighteen filled with dreams of *Dante* and *Beatrice* into a "Vita Nuova," a world so brightly yellow-green under a strangely darkening sky? Such was the madness of an April day. . . .Or had he heard something? From Raven perhaps? Or had he seen old Huthing the furnace man, he of the many children and listless wife, as he stood beyond the garden window with Flora the cook? His wrinkled face had bent laughing over her sallow face, and he had picked the blue scilla and put it in her heavy black hair. She had thrown back her head and, laughing, opened her mouth showing her blackened teeth.

"Blood of Hyacinthus," Raven sighed, and he walked out.

"Oh, Hyacinth? She never did any of those things. She made them up. Always loved to dramatize herself. A diseased mind. Liked to trade personalities, they say—created Hyacinth from and ancient legend she was in love with, the myth of Hyacinthus, wrote verse, a sonnet, I think. Seed of the tale perhaps."

"She created Hyacinth? Destroyed her too, perhaps? Say the lines to us!"

"I can't remember quite. . . ."

"Never knew her myself. Some sort of dancer, wasn't she? Singer, rather. Actress, perhaps? We moved in next door last month. Thought she was dead."

"Death! That was like it. I remember now. The words don't make much sense though:

'To burgeon now, long Hyacinthus bled,
And he who lived, flow'rs once again though dead.'"

"Who is that hideous old lady, then, scratching her bald head? that wild-eyed thing, blind, I think."

"Old? Why Hyacinth is only thirty or a little more; it couldn't be!"

"Well, that one there whom the young man is staring at from the dark room."

And then someone made an odd mistake. It was Madame.

She advanced. Her terrible face peered in at me. She was again a gigantic malevolent owl. Her great pointed mound of white hair, once so ridiculous, grew into towering feathers. She would fly at me, tearing my flesh with her claws and beak, blinking her heavy lids as she devoured me. I remembered a dream of the docile dark pigeons of St. Marks.

I had stood in Venice against a brilliant blue sky in ecstasy at the pigeons turned dazzling white in the overpowering sunlight, and, suddenly, they had fallen, a white storm from the sky, fierce gulls mistaking me for their prey. Wing upon wing and white against blue, they came screaming down the sky at me, and I awakened screaming too.

But this time when I awoke, the dream remained—a face hanging in mid-air like an ectoplasmic cloud—and I knew that I had been grinning back at it foolishly, frozen as the frightened rabbit in the field with the eagle overhead.

Then, abruptly, it drew back, dissolved, and I heard, moving into the distance, a voice that I had heard a moment before.

"I thought she was dead," it said. "I thought she was dead."

From high in the house, the parrot began screeching, "Yacinth! Yacinth! Yacinth!"

"Hyacinth, Hyacinth! You stupid parrot!" I screamed without making a sound.

That ridiculous, offensive, disgusting name!

THE SWEET BEYOND

Ah! Just as I had suspected, she was still at it: expurgating, re-arranging, glossing, re-coloring. The front yard was lavender-blue smoke from the distance a carpet of scilla sewn tightly as petit-point to the base of the house whose old pink brick had been freshly whitened, burgeoning minutiae of the foison of her discontent. Her smile would be as new as the face of the interior, chessman in the eternal dress rehearsal. "Marietta," she would say drawing back the door, "delightful." Her husband would rise halfway in his chair revealing a crescent of feeling which, however little, was yet too much.

How welcome at the ambiguous prospects was the last reassuring sense of life and freedom, the inward-outward double image of self, the gleeful snap of vanity against the pavement: red-calfed spikes, the bemused whim of a pink suit, the always charming uncertainties of future! Yet of certainties there were many more. The group would meet as in the past with the same ostensible purpose, each with his private curiosity, his personal malignancy.

Yet first, before descending into the tombs, a long breath of the sweet spring-sharp air, a white kid finger on the shattering bell. "Valentina!" I exclaimed at her scarlet and white print self: blood spilled on the great white wings of a moth . . . What delightful naturalism, Valentina! Poppies in a white cloud!"

"Mark adores it . . . We've been waiting for Lewyn. He'll expect to lead the group still, I suppose . . . so sensitive . . . slipping though; we've developed since you last came. You'll see." She turned the dark pyramid of her head expectantly.

The coffee walls and rust slipcovers had disappeared, last reminder of the first Mrs. Spink. Valentina had effaced them in a wash of pink ceiling to floor and the triumphant greenery of chartreuse modernism. The overstuffed easy chairs were no more, and amid the jungle of plastic and blond wood Mark Spink was to be observed a rueful pawn whose innocent smile I could somehow imagine turning sly in the darkened room of the seance below.

"Primavera! Enchanting," I assured her, but she had already turned her rapacious eyes upon the quasi-settled Mark who was surrounded by speci-mens of a stratum ordinarily inadmissible to her parlor: Mr. Bunker who turned his great colorless eyes upon me in imperceptible recognition, Miss Coone of the carnelian hair and swarthy skin, a rodent to his hippopotamus. Valentina pointed heavenward significantly, "Since Lewyn is appar-ently not to come—" but he had already slid in on her glissando, a fawn in crepe soles.

The metamorphosis had begun; one could sense it in the acceleration of rhythm, the inflating melodrama of speech, instinctive half-conscious orchestration to the percussion instrumentation of our feet as we descended the concrete spiral to the cellar room. It was cold and damp; Indian rugs hung from the walls and a black curtain annexed a corner. Valentina had seated us care-fully and to her purpose: Mark between herself and the informidable Miss Coone, myself be-tween Mr. Bunker and Lewyn, the male-female chain an intrinsic part of the design. "Lights out; join hands in your circle. All together, now, a good song to get the vibrations started." Her voice swooped up and we fell in, 'Put your head upon my boo-zum . . .'"

We were swaying in unison, metal chairs creak-ing, my hand aching in Mr. Bunker's great paw, the other tangled in Lewyn's cold skeletal fingers. One by one they recited what they saw, but I, as usual, could not see what they saw. I could hear and feel and smell: Mr. Bunker's vast flaccid leg edging me from my chair, his licorice breath, his sweating palm, but what I saw was guesswork. Lewyn held sway, triumphantly saw the most:

"I see a child in spirit; he says it was the pretty colored things that did it. Ah! That's it! That's it! Jelly beans! He choked to death on jelly beans on Easter day . . ." His voice fell an octave into a monotonous singsong, "Celine and Meline are here . . . send love to mother."

"Those horrid little foetuses again!" Did I imagine Miss Coone's voice across the room? Surely if I were to ask, they would claim it had been discarnate! Did I imagine, too, her face in the dark, its expression the same as the afternoon she had invited me to her apartment, her dark face bent over the cups as she poured tea as though on stage with charm, abandon, and malice?

"Valentina imagines those foetuses will hold Mark! What are they next to the real children of his first wife? Hah! And she thinks because you are younger and prettier than we she must keep you away from Mark! She thinks me without passion you know! What does she know of passion but jealousy? Let her conjure up all the foetuses she likes, let her repaint and throw out all the furniture that Helen bought; she'll never exorcise that one!" The foetuses were sending the usual pretty messages. The little room without ventilation had become a sweat-box, but Helen must come before it could be done, and she would address Valentina as tactfully, as soothingly as ever; and Valentina must pretend to see and Miss Coone rattle off her endless colors, her Jewels set in darkness. ("Low stage of development, that," Lewyn would mutter in my ear passing out the door.)

"Helen is here. She says she is often in the home" (happy thought!) . . . often, often in the home, wants to tell Valentina she is doing a good job." I could see no Helen but fancied a gleeful smile on Mark, could imagine Valentina glowering, turning the light on suddenly to catch him or did he, believing, squirm at the thought of Helen's nocturnal visits?

Later, when we were gone, would Valentina go about turning off the lights again, wondering where Helen was, following her and being followed, fearing her reality for Mark separating them from physical intimacy, from the very spiritual intimacy she both sought so avidly and feared?

"Your turn Mr. Bunker. What do you see to-night? One of the White Brotherhood stands over your head!"

Mr. Bunker's hand was relaxed, and he did not answer.

"He's in a trance!" It was Miss Coone's little shriek of delight or amusement. "He's in a trance," she said again. "Developing fast . . . only been sitting with the circle a little while, one of the White Brotherhood, a true sensitive!"

I thought of how recently the 'true sensitive's' exploratory fingers had been discouraged with difficulty.

"What have you been concealing, Mr. Bunker?" Miss Coone's voice was coy. In answer, there was a snort and then, unmistakably, a snore. At first they prenteded not to hear it,, but it grew into so dominant a roar they had begun to scream at each other to be heard. "And you, Marietta, did you see something tonight at last?" It was Valentina sounding for my position.

"No, no, still nothing," I cried. "The power is up. Time to go behind the curtain, Lewyn," said Mark and I could sense the hatred that must be in Valentina's face, but if anyone else felt her envy, her determination to play medium, none invited her. Lewyn's voice came out above the snoring; it was a groan, a wail and sounded peculiarly unlike him. He had taken on the voice of his spirit guide, Chief Dripping Water, whose guttural ungrammatical prose invariably began with a warning not to touch the medium while he was in trance.

"No touch medium; you frighten heem; he maybe die: No touch! No touch! No touch!"

"Who, what frightened Lewyn? His own imagination? That he might be caught cheating? I smiled and suddenly, unaccountably, I wept. They had begun to infect me with their folly. I would not come back.

And then the voice of a woman, Helen's voice as we had never heard it before—personal, compelling, feminine, deliberately beguiling, speaking to Mark as she had never had the indiscretion to speak before. She was reminiscing, evoking the nostalgia of the past: "Do you remember the first evening, Mark? The plum blossoms . . . we went swimming in the river . . . lost our way going home in the dark. Ah, how you could dance, Mark! There was never anything like you. I'm still rather fond of dancing. . . ." Suddenly the voice fell flat, became the old motherly tone so long concerned but for Valentina, "I'm often in the home, often in the home, in the home, in the home . . ." she ran down like an unwound old phonograph to a guttural scratch.

I began to wonder, idly, in what part of the house Helen might be found—the boudoir certainly!

I became aware that Mr. Bunker's snore had long since stopped, of a sodden silence. I forced my swollen feet back into my pumps edging away from Mr. Bunker's quickened and importunate leg, and standing up, fell through the hot bath to the faint smoky light coming through the closed door. It fell back as I leaned away pulling upon the knob and a sigh rushed past me as the light broke in.

I turned back and saw them sitting in the circle still. They were motionless, their faces yellowed Byzantine mosaics suspended in limbo. The black curtain was pulled back and Lewyn sat rigid in the oak chair, his eyes bulging in sightless fixity at the Sweet Beyond.

TO SLEEP AND TO WAKE

Despite her name (snatched from a romantic novel of the South which her mother had been reading when she was born), Melrose was born in the North so when Lolla came to work for her, she didn't know what to expect. There had been a colored woman in her childhood who did the washing and who seemed to belong vaguely to the cellar, a dusky fat and friendly ghost, but now she really didn't know what to say sometimes or how to act, and they were both uncomfortable.

Her neighbor, Mrs. Malmallow, had had a girl from the same camp of migrant workers, though.

"Look out!" Mrs. Malmallow had said when Melrose told her that she had hired her. "I'd think, after my experience, you'd never dare!"

"Well, you know how the help situation is," said Melrose embarrassed, "and she really looks very sweet and quiet—and clean!"

Mrs. Malmallow sniffed audibly, and Melrose knew what she was thinking and wished she'd not made a fool of herself by telling her anything.

Mrs. Malmallow triumphed by repeating her story of Susan. "Harrowing experience, really! That gigantic skinny creature! That endless fierce face! Murderous temper, too, she had! And those wildmen she called 'gentlemen callers!' That bushman-without-a-name who came into the house without a sound! Took off his hat once to scratch his scalp and his hair stood up all over eight inches long! Sure he was going to charge! That was the last straw for me, I tell you! And how she tried to intimidate me! She was forever asking to borrow money and telling me (what brass!) all that tremendous repertoire of mad tales! Could always banish the faintest signs of incredulity by pointing to that long deep wound in her right leg! Used to hint darkly she could shoot straight—even implying subtly she toted a gun!"

"This one looks pretty innocent, really," Melrose said hesitantly and went out the side door feeling depressed and ashamed.

It was almost time for dinner when Melrose got back and found Lolla in the pantry reading "True Love." Something smelled as though it were beginning to burn and she stepped awkwardly around Lolla to the stove and turned the

(48)

heat down under the hamburg and onions. She wanted to say something and thought better of it. Sam will tell me she's hopeless, she thought, and I thought she couldn't go wrong on hamburg!

After dinner, Lolla went out the back door. They heard the door close after voices, anyway.

"She's too silent for me," Sam said, the pipe stem snapping between his teeth. "When they don't talk, they DO—God knows what!"

"She talks to the children. I hear her laughing with them when they go into the kitchen after school. Perhaps she's afraid of us!"

"Afraid of you? Hunh! I notice she goes right on reading "Sexy Sagas" or doing her embroidery when you go out."

"I shouldn't have told you and you wouldn't have noticed!"

"How naive!"

So it went for many months as they wondered aloud when she had gone about what she really thought, whether she was really happy so isolated from her own people until her day off, yet they knew in their hearts that it could not be home to her.

Melrose always knew Wednesday by Lolla's singing in the laundry and her quickened smile. And she would never come back on time. From the time her little round face would go out smiling after assuring them that she would be back the following night, it was certain to be many days before she would reappear.

After a week or so, they would usually have to go to find her—parking their new green Buick out of sight of the hut and going towards it on foot self-consciously aware of making concessions to the awkwardness of contrast, telling themselves they were not doing it from curiosity.

"Strange she prefers that flimsy shack to our warm rooms for her," Sam said, but Melrose didn't answer because she knew he knew perfectly well why.

"Must be freezing in there on winter nights," Sam said kicking falling leaves aside from the little path through the abandoned apple orchard.

"Probably they'll go South again soon," said Melrose pulling her coat about her thin shoulders.

"Without any goodbyes of course," Sam added wryly.

He knocked on the door and there was a long silence and finally a man's voice asking, "Who's it?" Lolla finally appeared in a pair of tight blue jeans, a tight tee shirt over her great unbrassiered bust. She talked sleepily of female troubles and having to stay off her feet, "under doctor's care."

Later she moved in with them again. "She must have left Willy," Sam said one evening putting his great blond head against his fist on the mantel, his muscular face twisted humorously. "Probably fought over the chair we gave them. Maybe he wanted to sell it, great salesman with used shoes, you know. Well, at least she's not changed names again."

"Yes. I'm always afraid she'll pick something up and give it to the children—innocently, of course. The tub, the toilet, God knows how!"

One night in midwinter Sam was out of town and Melrose, shivering, went about the house locking every door and window as best she could. She hadn't the strength to turn all of the window locks, and the doors only reminded her of how easily determination would open them. Coming to the back door, she hesitated. What if Lolla should come back late and want to get in?

She remembered Sam shaking his head in that heavy rolling way of his saying, "It's her total unreliability I can't understand. If she'd bother to call when she's not coming, but it's that eternal silence of hers that gets me!" He stood with his back to her looking out the French doors at the darkening fields and she knew that he was thinking how foolishly fearful she would be while he was gone . . . and having doubts himself—remembering perhaps Mrs. Malmallow's tales of the sinister types she'd had to deal with.

It was true that their house was peculiar. It had been built by an architect of highly impractical nature who provided it with multiple colliding doors, ill-conceived chimneys that blinded with their smoke, and nine outer doors so successfully period that locks had been completely avoided except for tiny bolts that turned in eaten-away wooden holes. "Just spit on the French doors," Sam would say. "They'll invite you in."

This night he had turned to her, offering to teach her as he had so often before, the use of a pistol for self-defense. "Want me to show you how to use my Luger?"

"Good Lord! I couldn't, not even in self-defense," she protested for the nth time.

Melrose's excessive timidity made the nights especially fearful on wintry nights when the wind forced its way through the crevices of the flimsy house downstairs. Like Lolla's downstairs, she thought, and stood in her nightgown barefooted on the cold kitchen floor yearning for the warmth of the upstairs rooms. It must be near zero outside and she wondered where Lolla was in the terrible night. She put the light on on the back porch and scribbled a note on the chance that Lolla might pick this night to return to her upstairs room. She opened the door and slid the note over the door knob. "Dear Lolla," she had written, "Please ring the bell." The chill wind sent her backwards into the room as she bent to secure the note and her pink nightgown twisted backwards as she shook in the cold. She ran against the door slamming it and still lingered leaning against it fearful, afraid to go up to her bed leaving the door unlocked (those wildmen!) and afraid to lock it for fear Lolla might have to wait too long on the step while she came down to let her in. Oh but she would not come tonight and God knew who else might try the door! She turned the latch and ran upstairs as though pursued by demons from the shadows where she had but just then extinguished the light having seen nothing frightful.

It was a terror out of her girlhood—that dark old house in which she had been born where she had fled up the stairs after turning out the light. How she had tried to slow her feet by self-control! How fear had always won out over her in the end!

She stepped into each of the children's rooms bending over them, kissing them and smiling at their innocent closed faces.

I cannot stay up all night listening, she thought, as she stepped into her bed, and yet she lay there worrying for a long time. Once she thought she heard a sound at the back door, and she got up, quivering, and felt her way cautiously down the back stairs turning on lights as she went. She raised the red gingham curtain from the window on the back door and, looking out, saw the snow drifted glistening and without footprints on the porch.

What if Lolla should come back and I had fallen asleep? she thought. She would go back with the fellow who brought her, of course! Melrose stood frustrated by indecision. If only she could reach her and find her, know where she would be! But there was no phone near the shack.

Melrose went upstairs, the woolly staircarpet tickling her soles, going slowly at first and then faster, wildly, terrified by the unknown in pursuit. She lay down at last thinking: I'll be lying awake for hours, and if she is coming, it will surely be before I'm asleep. I'll surely hear her.

Suddenly, in the night, she heard a loud and terrifying sound, some nightmare's alarm clock, but when she looked at her clock, it was only six—hours too soon to get the children up for school. As the terrible current of horror screamed through her, she became slowly aware of its source howling from the pit of the house and she ran down the stairs pierced by the pain of terror and instinctive guilty foreboding.

As she came near the red curtains, she saw something orange between their parting, a shapeless form, and raising one side of the cloth, saw a figure leaning against the doorbell, a child's carriage robe thrown awkwardly over the head. To her horror, she recognized Lolla, her eyes closed and swollen; the terrible acid scars which she had never explained stood out incongruously in her childlike face. Was she dead? In the instant of horrified realization and paralysis, Melrose stared inwardly convicted, yet in the next she had opened the door and put her arm about her.

"Lolla! Lolla!" she cried in anguish, "How long have you been out there?"

She opened bloodshot eyes, and Melrose could see she had been weeping. "All night," she whispered hoarsely, her voice faint and quivering, "all night in your car."

"All night?" Melrose wept openly and unbelieving, unable to find words for her remorse, babbling foolishly, "How could you? Didn't you ring before?" Lolla nodded silently. "You should have

(55)

broken in, Lolla! Were you afraid? They're so flimsy, you know! The doors, I mean! My poor darling, did you think I valued those doors more than your life? If I hadn't left the car there by the back door would you have tried harder? You weren't afraid were you Lolla? Tell me! Tell me! You weren't afraid?" She could not stop talking, asking, pleading and despairing.

"Yes, I rang the bell," was all she could say, and Melrose helped her shivering up the stairs.

"Your bed won't warm you quickly enough. Come. I'll put you in mine and put the electric blanket on."

Lolla hesitated but was too weak to resist and lay down in her clothes.

"I'll be right back after I call the doctor," Melrose told her and ran down the stairs. He answered sleepily,

"Just try to keep her warm and I'll come."

Melrose hurried up the stairs wondering, anguished, what the night had done and knocked at the door, reticence returning.

"Please give me your foot. Rubbing may warm them more quickly." She saw with faint relief the many layers of clothing and thought of the irony of it. Her dressing for the little hut might have saved her life.

Lolla pushed her toes out from beneath the covers shyly and Melrose took off her several pairs of socks and began to rub her feet. They were stiff and icy between her hands and her toes were whitish.

What can I tell from the color of her skin, thought Melrose and wondered how she might dare ask about the white spots on her toes.

"Are they usually this color?" she asked at last aware of the awkwardness of the question and shuddering with the possibilities—what if her toes were frozen. Might she have to lose them? The thought of her responsibility struck Melrose more sharply than the ice that pierced her palm as it rubbed the roughened sole of Lolla's foot. The sole grew pink.

Suddenly she recalled something she had heard and drew her hand back so abruptly that Lolla stared.

"I just remembered, rubbing's just the wrong thing," and she stared at the foot. The color of mine, thought Melrose having forgotten the similarity and chagrinned at her own old unawareness.

"Do they tingle?" asked Melrose after Lolla had assured her that the white spots were only corns. They had both laughed then for the first time.

Yet Melrose kept asking her, "Do they tingle?" still fearful that the girl had suffered permanent damage.

"No. Just numb," she kept saying.

Melrose left her at last to get her a warm glass of milk and when she got back upstairs she found Lolla asleep her white scarf still tied turbanwise around her head and one hand against it her fingers twitching in her sleep. She was reminded, looking at her, of her children and went into the youngest's room who lay miraculously still asleep. As she kissed the soft warmth of his cheek he turned over smiling.

None of the children had awakened. Why had they not heard the bell while she had? My conscience, she thought and felt happy in the knowledge to find it even amidst her shame.

As she went downstairs into the still darkened room, she remembered how she had feared it so long, remembered the nightmares of her childhood in which a terrible and cruel man sat below in the shadows. How in her dream that she had had again and again she had known that the sight of him would kill her and yet that she must go down past him to the door although she had no courage to go but was forced somehow against her will.

She knew that she could never lock a door again with the same terror of the night, the same dread only for what might lurk outside ready to come in to devour her. The fear was reversed. She feared not her own death but that she would cause the death of another. Yet was it not all the same fear in the end? The door, the staircase? Were they not the same? A journey at long last alone where all men like to deceive themselves they need never go?

When it grew light, she went out to her car where she had left it in the driveway and could not get into the driver's seat. The door would not open, and she saw that in the long terror of the night, Lolla wrapped in the children's little carriage robe left carelessly in the car, had pressed down the lock on the inside.

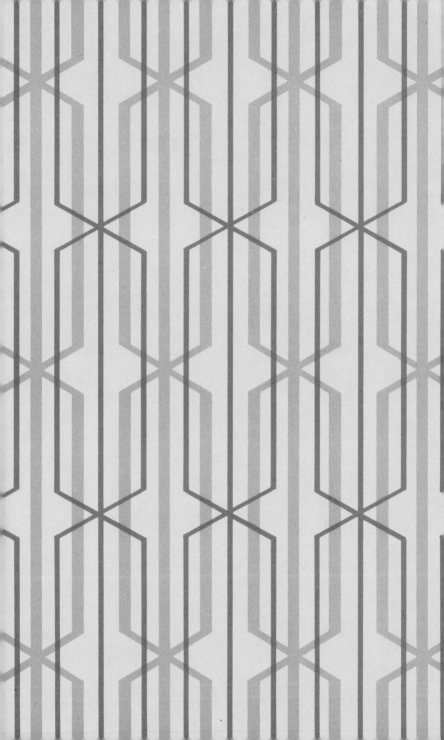